AF444925

# ECHO MOUNTAIN

## A Western Short Story

## J.C. HULSEY

**ACKNOWLEDGMENT**

TO MY CREATOR FOR GIVING ME
A BRAIN THAT WORKS LIKE MINE

## CHAPTER ONE

My name is Jarod Marsh. I was born in New York City, New York. My parents both died in an accident when I was ten. As an only relative, I went to live with my father's elderly uncle. When I was twelve, he said he was getting too old to take care of me, so he sent me to live in an orphanage. He said when I reached my majority, I would receive an inheritance that would be enough to set me up in any business I might want.

The years at the orphanage weren't the happiest years of my life, however, I did have a bed and three meals a day. I dreamt of the day when I would be old enough to leave this dreadful place. The day arrived when I turned eighteen. The director gave me a card with the name of a lawyer that was to give me my inheritance. I bid farewell to the others and to the caretakers and walked out the door with my merger belongings. I had no way of knowing which direction to go as I hadn't been outside the walls of the orphanage. I walked for what seemed like hours. Finally, I asked a man if he could direct me to the address on the card.

I approached the stranger on the street. "Excuse me sir. Could you direct me to the address on this card?"

"Why that place burned to the ground only a few weeks ago," he replied. "Everyone inside perished."

"Everyone, sir?" I asked. "Is there no one to conduct their business?"

"Not that I know about. As I said, everyone died in that fire."

What was I going to do now? The only things I had were the clothes on my back and a change of underwear in my satchel. I sat down on the sidewalk and placed my face in my hands.

"What's the matter, Laddie?" I looked up at an elderly gent with a kind face. "Why are you so glum?"

"I haven't any money." I said wiping my nose on my sleeve. "And I have no place to go"

"Where's your home?" he inquired. "Your parents?"

"I have no one. I've been living in the orphanage for six years. They turned me out because I'm now eighteen."

"How would you like to come home with me? I could use a young man like you to work in my stable."

"Truly sir? You would offer me employment?"

"That I am. Are you interested?"

"Are you an Angel? I had given up all hope and you come along. You must be an Angel."

"I'm no Angel. Far from it. I'm not an easy task master. You will be expected to work very hard."

"Oh yes sir. I will work very hard indeed."

Mr. Partinecel took me home with him and introduced me to Oscar Humphrey, who was the man in charge of the stables.

"Oscar, you've been needing some help for a while now. This is Jarod. I want you to teach him everything there is to know about the stables."

"Yes sir, I'll do that."

Oscar was a very good teacher and a very patient one as some things took me more than once to learn. He should be good; he had worked for Mr. Partinecel for over twenty-three years.

When I had been there a little over three years, Oscar passed away. After the funeral, Mr. Partinecel told me I was to have the same job that Oscar had held.

I worked for Mr. Partinecel for almost five years. He was, as he had warned, not an easy man to please. However, he did allow me time to learn the things that were required in my position.

He raised quarter horses for the very rich. People from around the world came to him for the best of the best horse flesh.

I had the opportunity to learn all there was to know about horses and became what some would classify as an expert.

Mr. And Mrs. Partinecel treated me as one of the family. I spent many evenings after supper visiting with them.

When I turned twenty-three, I decided I wanted to travel to California. I had heard how plentiful gold was there. It was said that one could bend down and pick it off the ground as you would pick vegetables. Mr. Partinecel said he was sorry to see me go, but he understood the wants and needs of a young lad such as me.

"Here is money you have earned while being in my employment. You put it in a safe place and use it wisely."

"Yes sir. I wasn't expecting this. I appreciate it very much."

"There is something else I want you to have."

"Oh no sir, you have given me quite enough."

"My wife and I have not been fortunate enough to have children and we consider you as one of the family, so I want you to have this watch. It belonged to my father and his father before him. I want you to have it with my blessings."

"But sir, I couldn't except it. It is much too nice and surely worth a lot of money."

"Please take it as a favor to me."

I reached and took this beautiful gold watch. When our hands touched, he took my hand in his and drew it to his chest and held it there for only a moment.

"Now be off with you and may the good Lord watch over you. Goodbye."

I packed my bags, of which I had a few more belongings than when I had left the orphanage. I bid him farewell and headed for the stage depot.

## CHAPTER TWO

While working for Mr. Partinecel, I had gone to town for only the few necessities I needed, such as new clothes and boots. I never stayed long and headed back to the ranch as soon as I was done. I arrived in town and headed for the stage station.

Stepping up to the ticket window I said, "One ticket to California, please?"

"Yes sir, but if I might make a suggestion. You would be a lot better off if you hooked up with a wagon train headed that way."

"Thank you, kind sir. Could you please direct me as to where I might accomplish this?"

"You're in luck. Mr. Shennagan, the Wagon Master is the one you need to see. He was in here this morning and said he would be signing on new folks at the Faraway Hotel. That's two streets over and one block east. Good luck to you."

"Thank you," I told him and hurried out the door. I found the Faraway Hotel and walked inside. There was a line of people waiting to meet with a gentleman seated at a desk. I observed what they were doing. He would ask them some questions. It seemed if he liked their answers, he would then take money from them and have them sign a paper. I got in line and waited my turn.

"Good day to you, young man. Are you wanting to go to California?"

"Yes sir. I am."

"Have you got a wagon and team? And is it outfitted for the trip?"

"No sir. I didn't know about needing anything," with a questioning look on my face. "I thought all I had to do was sign the paper and you would take me there."

"You're a real greenhorn ain't you?" he chuckled.

"A greenhorn, Sir?" I said. "I don't believe I am Sir. I'm Irish through and through."

"Aye. You are that. I tell you what Laddie. I'm in a good mood today. I be needing somebody to help with the animals. You know anything about horses and cows?"

"I do Sir. I have been a stable hand for Mr. Partinecel for almost five years. You can check with him for references, if you please?"

"That's alright. I'll take your word for it. You be here in the morning with your gear. Don't look so worried, here's a list of everything you'll need. As I said, you be here in the morning at six a.m. Don't be late. I don't want to regret hiring you. Now move along. There are others that want to travel with us."

~~~~~~~

The day we left was a cloudless sky of a deep blue color. The north wind was blowing a cool breeze and everyone had to wear a jacket. There were twenty-four wagons in the train. I won't list the things that were on the list that Mr. Shennagan gave me. I will say that it was a very long list and took almost half my money. There was an extra wagon that carried all the Wagon Master's goods and extras that might have to be replaced on the trail.
~~~~~~~

Mr. Shennagan, Mr. Green, the scout and myself would eat the supper meals with different folks each night. Each morning we would grab a cup of coffee and a biscuit from the same family we had eaten supper with. We didn't have a noon meal.

I became very fond of one family, well, maybe not the family so much as the daughter. Mary Beth Henderson had long blonde hair that shined like polished gold, and a smile that lit up the whole campsite when she smiled. There was only one small problem. I was so shy that I didn't say anything to her. Mr. Shennagan teased me about her whenever we had our meals with the family.

Mr. Shennagan was barking out orders like a Military Officer. I found out later that he had been a captain in the war. He had already told me to keep the horses and mules in a group until we got out on the trail and then we could loosen up a bit on controlling them. This was a lot different than what I had been doing for the last five years, however, I was a fast learner and caught on to my responsibilities very quickly.

We traveled approximately eight miles a day. The wagons were pulled by oxen which were used because they could pull heavy loads. They could survive on eating the grass along the way. They, also, didn't cost as much as mules.

There was a lot of comradery with the folks. Laughing and talking. Kids running wild. That is until we had been traveling for a week. Then tempers began to flare. A lot of the same people that were laughing and talking before were now in a foul mood. Oh they were still talking, but they weren't saying nice things to one another.

Mr. Shennagan would ride his big black stallion up and down the wagons and try to get folks to settle in.

"We still got a very long trip ahead of us." He would tell them. "There's no reason for you to be getting upset now. Save it for the savages if we're unlucky enough to meet up with them.

"You mean Indians?" a very large woman asked. "Are they going to attack us?"

"I can't answer that question," answered Shennagan. "However, if they were to attack, I wouldn't want to be at odds with my neighbor who might have to save my life. Now, stop acting like spoiled children and act like grown men and women."

That little talk did the trick. Folks apologized and got back to talking and laughing.

After the kids had school for a while, they had to gather buffalo chips. (Buffalo chips were the hardened manure droppings of the buffalo that could be used for fuel.) The children weren't very happy about that job. It was, however, easier than chopping wood each time we stopped.

At night we slept in or under the wagons. Some slept in a tent and some slept out under the stars.

Campfires were built and food was cooked in iron pots and skillets. Many times, meals were cooked only in the evening, and the cold leftovers were eaten for breakfast and the noon meal, as we didn't always stop for a noon meal.

Food that wouldn't spoil along the way was taken. Beans and rice, dried meat and salted bacon, dried fruit, hardtack or crackers (hard dried bread which had to be softened in water to eat). Flour and sugar and sometimes baked bread, biscuits, or pies. We would drink coffee and tea, and sometimes lemonade would be made with lemon extract. Many families took along a milk cow to have fresh milk and butter along the way. As we traveled, folks would hunt and fish along the way for antelope, buffalo, deer, elk, rabbit, birds, and trout.

I wanted to go hunting, but Mr. Shennagan said I was needed to take care of things in camp.

"Besides?" he asked. "Have you ever fired a rifle?"

"No sir, but I'm willing to learn," I told him proudly."

"When the men leave the train to go hunting, they're leaving it unprotected while they're gone," He explained. "They wouldn't have time for a greenhorn such as yourself. You stay in camp, where you're needed. However, when Hiram Green gets back, he can teach you how to handle a rifle. But, tomorrow, you'll be driving the lead wagon."

"But I've never driven a wagon."

"You're a fast learner. You'll be driving like a mule skinner before you know."

"What's a mule skinner?"

"You greenhorn!" he guffawed as he rode away.

I had been riding a horse taking care of the stock. What was it like to ride in a covered wagon?

Bumpy! The sturdy wagons had no springs, and the roads were not smooth, but were full of potholes and rocks. Every time the big wheels rolled over a bump, everything in the wagon got bounced and jostled. The dirt roads were muddy when it rained, and dusty when it didn't rain. Most of the people walked, and only rode in the wagon when tired or sick. I envied the men who were riding horses. My insides felt all jumbled up. A few days later, I realized I had had it easy riding horseback.

Each evening after the meal was finished, Mr. Green, (He was the scout for the wagon train) would teach me how to shoot a rifle. I must admit it was like Mr. Shennagan had said. I was a quick learner. I could shoot the rifle so well that Mr. Green taught me how to handle and shoot a pistol. "I ain't never seen nobody learn how to shoot so quick. You're what folks call a natural."

I thanked him and asked, "If I may be so bold, perhaps you might teach be to a scout?"

"It would be my honor, young man." However, that would not happen because after fifteen days of traveling, we were attacked by Indians, I was the only survivor.

When they attacked, I had never heard such blood curdling sounds. I, also, heard the people I had been traveling with as they screamed and cried. What I suppose hurt the most was hearing the children's screams.

I jumped from the wagon completely forgetting the rifle I had worked so hard to learn how to use, it was left leaning against the wagon seat. I started running toward a rocky ravine.

I was almost there when I felt a thud just below my right shoulder blade and an immediate hot burning sensation in the middle of my back. The pain was excruciating and then my whole back went numb. It crept from my back to the top of my head and then all the way down to the tips of my toes and then back again, yet I somehow stayed on my feet. I felt a second projectile enter just to the left of the first one. This one knocked me down with a force that I can't describe. I was lying on the ground with my face in the dirt and I couldn't move. The pain was indescribable. I had had minor injuries in the past, but they were nothing to compare to this. I could still hear the mournful cries of my fellow travelers, but not for long, because the darkness closed in on me. I had no more control over it than a new-born baby trying to walk.

## CHAPTER THREE

I woke up. At least I thought I was awake.

I could hear voices somewhere far away. There were two people. A man and a woman. I could hear them talking about someone dying. *Was I dying? If I could hear them, surely I wasn't dying. Maybe if I say something.*

"Did he speak?" asked the male voice.

"I not hear nothing," said the female.

"I think he spoke," he said.

"Him bad shape. Don't think him speak, never again."

*No. I'm not dead. I'm right here. Please. You've got to hear me. I don't want to die. Please listen to me.*

"There. I heard him again," said the male.

"You right. Me hear too."

"I'll give him drink of water," he said. "I don't know how he's lasted this long with two arrows in his back."

"Great Spirit keep him alive for reason we not know," said the female.

"I don't think your great spirit had anything to do with keeping him alive. I think it was sheer determination and willpower on his part that's kept him alive. He's the only person out of the whole wagon train that's still breathing. He still might not make it. I figure if we can get some liquid in him, he will have a fair chance of staying alive."

~~~~~~

My voice seemed to stick in my throat. I needed to tell them that I'm not dead. But I couldn't speak. I did, however, make a guttural sound.

"There. I know you heard that," argued the man.

"Me hear. Him not dead," she said. "Not yet."

"Help turn him on his side so I can try to get some water in him. Can't turn him all the way over until those arrows come out."

I groaned as they turned me on my side and then I felt the cool liquid slide down my parched throat. Then I groaned again as they turned me back on my stomach.
~~~~~~

"Not pull out arrows 'till ready. Him bleed much."

"Build a fire," he told her. "We need to cauterize the wounds as soon as we pull them out."

"I gather wood for fire." I heard her shuffle away.

"Let me have your knife," he said when she returned. "So we'll have one for each wound. I'll stick'em in the fire. When they're hot enough, I'll hold him while you pull out the arrows one at a time and place the hot knife against the wound searing it closed. Then we'll repeat the same thing on the other one."

I would have screamed if I could have. However, I couldn't do more than grunt and moan and I did a lot of that.

"Now pour some whiskey on'em and wrap'em up. If they don't get infected, he's got a fair chance."

~~~~~~

I don't know how long I was unconscious, but as I opened my eyes, I could see the cloudless sky was a deep blue color. The north wind was blowing a cool breeze
~~~~~~

through the open window. It was a welcome relief from the heat of the fever that had ravaged my body.

"Can you drink a little water?" the man asked as he raised me up enough so I could sip from the tin cup. It trickled down my dry throat cooling as it went down.

"That's enough for now," he said laying me back. "You can have more in a little while. Are you able to speak?" he asked.

I tried to speak, but I couldn't utter a word. I tried again. No sound other than a muffled mutter.

"That's okay, in a day or so we'll take you to the doctor. "He'll find out what's wrong and why you can't talk."

I learned the names of my benefactors were Bearclaw and Moonglow. Bearclaw was what was referred to as a Mountain Man. He had lived, hunted and trapped these mountains for going on 50 years. Moonglow was his Indian wife.

In the days after they removed the arrows from my back, even though I couldn't speak, I learned about their lives. Bearclaw's life as a young man wasn't that much different than mine. He had left civilization at a young age on a whim that he wanted to be a trapper. While trapping in the mountains, he met and married Moonglow.

~~~~~~

"She was the most beautiful woman I had ever laid eyes on," he said with love in his voice. "I knew the moment I laid eyes on her, I wanted to marry her. I reckon she's still beautiful, but don't you go telling her I said so."

When they both tried to move into a small community, the people rejected them calling him a squaw man and calling Moonglow a dirty dog eatin' Injun. People can be awfully mean sometimes without even trying. Bearclaw decided since civilization didn't want him, he would live out his life with his bride in the mountains.

The more we visited, the more I grew to love both of them.

One day Bearclaw said to me, "I reckon we'll take you to the doctor's tomorrow. Are you ready to go?"
~~~~~~

I nodded my head that I was.

The next morning Bearclaw and Moonglow loaded me on a travois and we headed to the doctor's office. The swaying motion of the travois pulling behind Moonglow's horse put me to sleep. I would have liked to have stayed awake to enjoy the luscious green scenery.

## CHAPTER FOUR

When we arrived at the doctor's office in a small town, he was very busy with an epidemic of some kind, so Bearclaw and Moonglow stayed and helped until nurse Thatcher showed up. Then the trapper and his wife left to go back to their home on Echo Mountain.

Moonglow touched my hand with her wrinkled one as she looked deep into my eyes. I thought I saw a glimmer of tears in her eyes, but it couldn't be, because I had always heard that Indians don't show their emotions. She released my hand, turned and left the room.

Bearclaw said, "When you get up and around, why don't you come and stay with the old woman and me for a spell. I believe you would enjoy yourself. Heck, that's not the only reason I want you to come. The Creator never seen fit to bless me and my old woman with kids. We've both become real fond of you and would consider it a blessing if you would come, fer a while, anyhow. Think on it while you're mending. God bless, Son. You keep yer powder dry," he touched my hand, turned and walked out the door.

It was a sad day for me. I was going to miss them with all my heart. Maybe I would take him up on his offer and go stay with them for a spell.

~~~~~~

The dust flew in the open windows and spread a film of dirt on the floor, the furniture and everything in sight. I pulled the cover up over my nose to get a small amount of relief.

There was a woman standing in front of the window blocking out the cool breeze that was blowing through it. She, also, blocked out most of the light provided by the morning sun.

She had blonde hair with brilliant green eyes that seemed to look into my soul. She was not a beautiful woman, yet she wasn't not pretty. She was what one would call a handsome woman. Her blonde hair released a tiny curl that fell across her forehead. She reached with her hand, large hands for a woman, and brushed it back. She leaned close and spoke as if conversing with a child.
~~~~~~

"How are we feeling today? Can you talk? I'm the doctor's nurse in these parts. I believe you might live after all. It was touch and go for a while, but Bearclaw and Moonglow have taken very good care of you. You would have certainly died had they not removed those arrows. Now roll onto your side and let me take a look?"

When she leaned close to me, I smelled a clean soapy smell and the scent of lilacs. She raised the bandage up and probed with her fingers.

"The wounds are healing nicely. You should be able to get out of bed in a few days. Now. Lie down on your back again. I want to take a look at your throat. There has to be a reason why you aren't able to speak."

I lay on my back and looked up at her. The more I looked at her, the better looking she became.

She touched my throat with both hands, gently pressing with her fingers.

"I can't find any injury. Try swallowing while I press here." I swallowed and it felt like a rock was going down my throat.

"I think you must have hit your throat on something when you fell. If it doesn't get better in a couple of days, I think Doctor Montgomery should take a look. Right now, I recommend not trying to talk. Let it rest and heal itself. I'll be back to see you in a few days. If you feel you're strong enough, then by all means try to sit up. Don't try to get out of bed yet. You could break those wounds open, then we'd be back to square one. We don't want that. See you in a few days."

She turned and I was surprised. She had a very womanly figure. She was wearing a white dress with a high collar that swayed when she walked. She was carrying a small valise like a doctor's bag. She turned and looked at me as she opened the door. She was beautiful. She looked like an Angel standing silhouetted in the doorway. She stepped through and pulled the door closed behind her.

I lay there quietly contemplating my situation. The door opened again. I looked expecting to see her again. Her. I don't even know her name. Did she tell me and I forgot?

~~~~~~

The person who came through the door was Moonglow.

*'I thought you left,'* I mouthed the words and looked surprised.

"You feel better now. Nurse say you doing real good. Maybe get out a bed in two maybe three days. She say you no try to speak. You want something to eat. You feel much better after food. I go bring soup for you. Wild turnip soup. Very good. I make special for you."

She left and returned with a big bowl and a spoon. I tried to sit up but was too weak.

"You stay down. I feed you. Open mouth. One spoon at a time. That's good. Here, another."

She fed me like a baby. The soup was very tasty. I could feel the nourishment as it coursed through my body. I nodded my head and mouthed a thank you to the old woman. She nodded, then left the room.

I was again alone with my thoughts. *What was I going to do now? All my belongings, everything I owned in this*
~~~~~~

*world was gone. I guess I should look on the bright side of my predicament. At least I'm alive. What about the other folks on the train. Did any of them survive? Am I the only survivor? And if so, why me. What does God have in store for me. Surely He has something, or I wouldn't be lying in this bed.*

The days passed slowly. I counted three sunrises. *Where was she? Where was Nurse Thatcher? She said she would come back in a few days. How many days is a few? Moonglow has been feeding me turnip soup every day. I am feeling stronger, but still am not able to sit up. I wanted so much to show her I'm getting better. I want to sit up in bed for her. Another day has passed and she still hasn't come. Maybe she has forgotten me.*

## CHAPTER FIVE

The door opened.

"Hello, Pilgrim," it was Bearclaw. "You doing any better? I've been out running the trap line. Got some fine pelts. Also got some meat so you can stop eating Moonglow's soup. How's that sound?"

I nodded in the affirmative.

"I knew you'd like that. You want some water?"

I nodded again.

"You wanna try to sit up to drink it?"

I nodded.

"Let me get you started and then you come on up on your own."

I gripped his offered hand and pulled. He started pulling and I was sitting up. I thought my face was going to crack I was smiling so big.

"Now, let's let you back down," he held my hand and I was lowered onto my back again.

"Ya done real good." He said. We visited for a while before he said he'd better get back. "The old woman's waiting and if there's one thing she don't like is waitin'. Don't forget now, yer gonna come visit when yer up and around."

I nodded my head and Bearclaw patted my hand, then turned and left.

A couple days later, both Moonglow and Bearclaw came into the room.

"Well, we're really leaving this time. I reckon you're wondering why we didn't leave like we said last time. Well, we figured since the nurse checked you and then she left for another patient, we better watch out fer you. After all, we got a little bit of time invested in you. But we just seen the doctor and he's gonna be showing up anytime now, so we gotta git back up yonder. Now you 'member what I asked you. When yer feeling up to it, come fer a visit. We're located just in the foothills, ya just veer to the right of the trail and ya can't miss us." They both reached and clasped my hand, then they were gone.

~~~~~~

I spent the rest of the day sitting up on my own and then sitting on the edge of the bed with my feet hanging down.

The next morning early, a stocky middle-aged man with thinning gray hair wearing wire rimmed glasses came into the room.

"Good morning, young man. I'm Doctor Montgomery. Nurse Thatcher tells me you may have an injured larynx. Are you able to sit up?"

I nodded.

"Please sit up." He placed both hands just like the nurse did and pressed easily. "Now. Swallow. Uhhu. I don't feel any damage. Why not try to speak? Wait? I'll get you some water. That'll help for your dry throat." He poured a glass full and handed it to me. I put it to my lips and took a small sip. "Go ahead. Take a big one. We want it lubricated all the way down." I took two big swallows. "Now. Talk to me."
~~~~~~

"Hellloo." I squeaked. It had been a while since any sound other than a grunt or a groan had passed these lips. "I uh. I'm talking."

"Does it hurt anyplace?" the doctor continued to press and feel my throat.

"No sir," I answered grateful that I could answer. "It feels fine. A little dry, but otherwise it's fine. I'm really talking."

"There's no pain when you swallow or when you speak?" as he straightened.

"No. It feels great. I was beginning to think I would never speak again. But. I'm talking and it feels wonderful. Thank you, Doctor."

"Don't thank me. Thank Bearclaw and Moonglow and of course Nurse Thatcher. Those are the people who deserve your gratitude. The way they removed the arrows and cauterized the wounds probably saved your life. Which by the way, they are healing nicely."

"May I ask where Nurse Thatcher is today? I was expecting her to return to see me."

"She's busy with another patient. One much worse than you were at your worst. There's no need for her to come back to see you as you're doing much better. Have you gotten out of bed yet?"

"I've been sitting on the edge of the bed with my feet hanging down. I think I might try to take a step."

"Don't push yourself too hard. Your strength will return. It's just going to take a little time. You must be patience. Now, I must bid you farewell. I have two more patients today and I'm behind schedule as usual."

"So, I should try to get out of bed on my own?" I asked as he stopped at the door.

"No, no, don't try it by yourself, you're still much too weak for that. There will be someone to help you either today or first thing in the morning," he pulled the door closed.

~~~~~~

Later that afternoon the door opened, and a young lady came in. I had forgotten that I could speak now and before I realized it, I said aloud, "My, you are beautiful."
~~~~~~

She blushed, her cheeks flushing her pale white skin a crimson red. She was a slender girl and was tall for a female. Her brown hair was curly and little ringlets kept slipping across her forehead. She was a very pretty woman, even more so than Nurse Thatcher, but somehow, she didn't illicit the same response from me as Nurse Thatcher had. Her expressive blue eyes seemed to hint that she might be lonely.

"Hello, my name is Maggie Cole. I'm here at the request of Nurse Imogene Thatcher."

*So, that's her name. I'm not too fond of it, but it's a nice name for a nice lady.*

"Is Nurse Thatcher gonna be coming later?" I asked her, fiddling with the covers.

"I really can't answer that question. She's the head nurse in the territory and is extremely busy all the time. I should be able to care for you as well as her. Now, have you been able to get out of bed any at all?"

"I stood on my own yesterday, but not very long. I seem to give out easily," I explained.

"You'll regain your strength in time. Don't try to rush it."

Nurse Thatcher had struck me as someone who wouldn't shirk her duty no matter what the reason.

"Miss Cole?"

"Yes?"

"Is Nurse Thatcher married?"

"No. Unless you'd call her work a spouse. She's married to her work. Why do you ask?"

"No reason. Just thinking out loud."

"Alright, let's have a go at getting you out of that bed. You ready?"

"I sure am. Do you think you'll be able to hold me if I fall?"

"I'm a lot stronger than I look. However, if you feel you're going to fall, give me a warning. I think I'll be able to handle you."

It gave me an odd feeling when I placed my arm around her shoulder. However, I soon overcame that with the exertion I had to put into taking a few steps.

"I think that's enough for today. Let's get you back under the covers."

When I was settled back in the bed, I said to her, "Boy I'm pooped. I didn't realize how weak I had become."

"Just give it time. You'll be good as new in a few months," she said, pulling the cover up to my chin. "You'll be wondering if this was just a dream. Now, what would you like for supper?"

"Please no more soup," I begged her in my squeakiest voice.

"No more soup. I promise," she laughed. How would you like a venison steak? Bearclaw left some before he left. He said to be sure that you eat plenty of meat to build up your strength."

I had forgotten how real food tasted. However, I did fill my shrunken stomach very quickly.

Miss Cole came back for the dish and saw I had only eaten about half of it. "Don't worry, your stomach will stretch to accommodate much more as you recuperate."

The next few days seemed to rush by with me getting out of bed and walking, then eating another meal of fresh meat. I was beginning to feel like my old self.

Maggie and I had become friends during this time. She talked to me about how the Lord must have something important for me to do with my life, or He wouldn't have saved me.

"What in the world would He want me to do. I'm nobody, just a greenhorn as Mr. Shennagan used to call me."

"I'm sure you're more than that to God. In fact, we're all very special in His eyes. Did you know that He gave His only Son to die that we might live with Him in Heaven. Doesn't that sound great?"

"Yes, it does sound great."

"All you have to do is tell your God you're a sinner and you accept Jesus as your Savior."

"That's all? It sounds too easy."

"It is easy because God loves us and wants it to be easy."

~~~~~~

She told me about her family, about how her papa wanted her to marry someone important. "But I'm in love with a farmer," she said tearfully. "He doesn't have any money at all, but I love him and he loves me. What am I going to do?"

How could I give her advice? The only experience I had with women is what little time I had was my time spent with her and my infatuation with Nurse Thatcher. However, I, just like most people did have some advice for her.

"I think you should do what your heart tells you to do. As for your father approving or disapproving of the mate you choose should have no bearing on what you decide. You are the one that will be marrying this person, not your father. Of course, we all want to try to please our parents, but we can't always do that. Follow your heart," I reiterated.

"Oh, thank you so much for telling me that. I have been so worried about what my father thought, I forgot
~~~~~~

that I am the one that will live with my husband for the rest of my life, not my father."

## CHAPTER SIX

As my healing progressed, I began to think about what Bearclaw had asked me. As soon as the doctor said I was okay to make the trip, I was going to visit my good friends on Echo Mountain.

Almost six months to the day of getting injured, the doctor said, "All you need now is clean fresh air and continue to eat as you have been. I hope you realize how close you came to parting this world. May God bless you in the future as He has during this troubled time."

As I was dressing to leave. The doctor had provided me with a change of clothing. We had talked about what I might do after I was healed. She agreed that I should visit with Bearclaw and Moonglow.

"But," she said, "I think you should look for Nurse Thatcher first and tell her about your feelings for her. I have the distinct feeling that she is very lonely and that is probably the reason she stays so busy and works so hard. She told me quite a bit about you when she assigned me this job. More than she ever told me about other patients. Therefore, I think she, also, feels something for you."

"If she cared for me, then why hasn't she returned to see me?" I asked.

"Now, I don't know for sure," she confided. "But I think she may have had her heart broken at some time and she just doesn't want to get involved and risk another broken heart. I personally feel like you should approach her with your feelings. The worst she can do is reject your feelings. Even if she did, would you be any worse off than you are now?"

"Thank you for being a friend. I do believe I'm going to take your advice. Could you tell me where she might be this time of the month?"

"Yes, she should be right here in town. She has a regular patient here. You might check with Mrs. Ramsey at the general store. I, also, want to thank you for being my friend. If you're around in the middle of June, I want you to come to my wedding. Until I see you again, do you mind if I kiss you?"

"I would be honored to come to your wedding and I would love for you to kiss me."

She placed a gentle kiss on my cheek. It was just what I needed to raise my spirits.

"Here is something I want to give you."

She handed me a small Bible. "This can help you if you heed the words." We continued to visit as I grew stronger. Then one day, she said to me, "well, Jarod, I think you're ready to go out into the world and make your mark. You've been a dear friend and I'll never forget you. I want to wish me a speedy journey."

~~~~~~

I had only the items from the pockets of the clothes I was wearing when the Indians attacked. Bearclaw had saved them for me. In those meager belongings was a small pouch with my savings and the watch given to me by Mr. Partinecel. It wasn't much, but perhaps it would help until I could earn more. I shoved the bag into my pocket, bid farewell to Maggie and headed out on my journey. A journey that would change my life.

~~~~~~

I walked the couple of blocks from the doctor's office to town. A scruffy looking man was standing on the sidewalk in front of Ramsey's Dry Goods Store. He just stood and stared as I passed him and went into the store.

I stepped through the doorway and saw a heavy-set woman standing behind the counter. My boot heels echoed on the wooden floor.

"Mrs. Ramsey?" I asked the woman.

"Yes. May I help you?" as she looked me up and down.

"I'm looking for a woman," I said and her eyebrows raised. "She's a nurse," I continued.

"Are you the young man who's been laid up at the doctors?" she asked.

"Yes, Ma'am. My name is Jarod Marsh. I had a nurse named Thatcher when I first arrived. She promised she would return to check on me. She has not returned. I was hoping to locate her. Do you know her whereabouts?"

"Oh my. I'm so sorry to be the one to tell you this, but Nurse Thatcher died just this morning."

I felt as if I had been punched in the stomach as I found it extremely hard to breathe.

Mrs. Ramsey rushed from behind the counter. "Are you alright? Do I need to go for the doctor?"

I sat on a barrel there at in front of the counter. "May I just sit for a moment? I asked her.

"Of course. I'll go in the back and bring you some water. You rest easy."

She came back with a tall glass filled with cool refreshing liquid.

"You're looking much better. You color has returned. Here drink this," she handed me the glass.

"Thank you," I drank it down in one gulp and handed it back. "Can you please tell me what happened?"

"She was rushing to a patient. You know how she was, always in a hurry. Her patients were very important to her. Anyway, she was crossing the street when four cowhands came riding their horses into town like their tails were on fire. As they rounded the corner, there was poor Nurse Thatcher right there. There was no way for the cowboys to stop their animals and Nurse Thatcher couldn't get out of the way. Poor thing. At least she didn't suffer."

"I don't know what to say. I wanted so much to share my feelings with her about something that's been on my mind for some time now."

My heart was broken into a million pieces. My love was gone without her ever knowing how I felt. It seemed as if a voice inside me whispered, *Life must go on. There will be someone else later.*

"I'm so sorry, would you care for some more water?"

"No thank you, but I do need to do a little shopping while I'm here. Would that be alright?

"Of course, after all this is a store," she tried to make me feel more comfortable. "What will you be needing?"

"I will be making a trip into the mountains. I'm really not sure what I need. Perhaps you could help me?"

"Of course, I'll be glad to. Now first of all, you'll need a heavy coat.

"You're going to need a pack animal to carry all this stuff. Do you have one?"

"No, I hadn't given any thought as to how I was going to carry it."

"You can probably get a good one at the livery stable. Mr. Judson is a good man. He will treat you right. By the way, will you be attending Nurse Thatcher funeral?"

"Yes of course. When is it going to be?"

"I believe it will be day after tomorrow."

"Is it alright to leave my purchases here until I get an animal?"

"Absolutely, just leave them right where they are. What are you planning on doing up on the mountain, if I may ask?"

"I'm going to visit some friends. They asked me to come. I don't have anything to keep me here, not now, so this seems like the perfect time."

"I wish you a safe trip."

"Good day to you ma'am, you've been very kind to a stranger. Somehow you don't seem like a stranger. There is something about you that stands out and makes you feel like a friend."

"The livery stable is just up the street on the left. As said, I just know Mr. Judson will treat you right. Your supplies will be here waiting to be loaded on your animals."

I walked out of the store and to the livery stable. I walked inside and an old man with grey hair sticking from beneath a sloppy felt hat, wearing a strained grey shirt and bubble overalls stopped brushing a red sorel and turned to face me.

"Howdy young man, name's Hyram Judson, can I help you with something? Say, ain't you that young feller that was rescued by Bearclaw and Moonglow?"

"Yes, I am. Jarrod Marsh is my name and I'm wanting to purchase a horse so I can go visit them. Do you have a good one?"

"Sure do. Follow me." He turned and headed to the back door. "Got some fine thoroughbreds back here." He stopped at a small corral with six horses in it.

"I think I like that brown bay. She's looks to be a good one."

"You know yer horses alright."

"Yes sir. I worked for Mr. Partinecel in his stable for almost five years."

"You did say you're gonna visit Bearclaw up on Echo Mountain?"

"That's right. As soon as I attend a funeral."

"Nurse Thatcher huh, I plan on going myself. She was a very special person, to almost everybody. You plan on leaving right after?"

"Yes, there's not anything to keep me here."

"Well then, you're gonna need a horse that handles the mountain air and yer in luck, 'cause I got just the animal fer ya. Took her in trade just yesterday from a soldier just mustered out. Normally, soldiers don't git rid of their mounts, even retired ones, but he said he was in a bind and needed the money."

He pointed to another small corral holding the most beautiful Palomino that I had ever saw.

"He's beautiful." I said. "But there's no way I could afford an animal like that."

"How do you know. I ain't told you how much I want yet."

"Well, don't keep me in suspense. How much do you want?"

"Well now, ya said yerself she was a fine animal. How's fifty dollars sound?"

"That sounds okay, but I don't have that much."

"I'm sorry too, but I can't go any cheaper. Mighty sorry."

I scratched my head and thought. "Would you consider a trade?"

"Maybe. Whatcha got in mind?"

I reached into my pocket and removed Mr. Partinecel's watch. I hated to part with it, however, I was going to need a horse. A good horse.

"Let me take a look at that." He literally grabbed it, put it to his ear and a big smile appeared on his face.

"Had one like this once. Lost it on a trip. How much you figger you want fer it?"

"I wouldn't even begin to tell you your business. You tell me."

"I figger we got a trade and I'll even throw in a saddle, but you're gonna need a pack animal and I got just what you need."

"I don't have but one watch."

"It's okay, I'm just thankful to get this watch, I'm gonna let you have a complete setup to go and visit your friends. I can't tell you what it means to get my watch back. Oh, I know it ain't really the same watch, but it's close enough."

## CHAPTER SEVEN

The sky was overcast and dark, however, it looked like the whole town turned out for Nurse Thatcher's funeral. Even Maggie Cole was there. We spoke briefly, she said she was late to meet with a patient, so we said our goodbyes. I saw Mrs. Ramsey and told her I would see her back at the store.

After the coffin was lowered into the ground and the folks had all left, I stood there with my head bowed. I wanted to say something, but my throat felt like it had a knot in it. Finally, I whispered, "I wish I could have told you how I felt. I think you were the most beautiful person I have ever had the pleasure of knowing."

I turned and walked away with a heavy heart, but then, just as before in the general store, a feeling of calmness came over me and a still small voice whispered in my ear, *you will find someone else.*

I walked back to the livery stable to start on my journey to visit my friends.

~~~~~~
~~~~~~

Mr. Judson had provided me with a horse and tack, and a mule to carry all my goods. Things seem to be going good for me.

I gave Mr. Judson a heartfelt thank you and started leading my animals back to Mrs. Ramsey's store.

"I see you and Mr. Judson came to an agreement. That is a beautiful animal and I see you, also, have a mule to carry your supplies. While you were gone, I remembered something you will need. Maybe the most important thing. Don't know why I didn't think of it before."

"Don't keep me wondering. What is it?"

"Guns. You're going to need guns. A rifle and a handgun. A Hawken rifle and a pistol should be alright. And how about a couple of knives?"

"That all sounds fine, but am I going to have enough money to pay for it?"

"I'm sure you'll be fine."

When everything was tallied up, it was a lot less than I expected. In fact, I had money left over.

"Let's get these things on the animals. I'm sure you're in a hurry to get on the trail. The sooner you leave the sooner you'll get there."

When we had the goods loaded and tied down, I turned to Mrs. Ramsey. "I'm finding it hard to say goodbye to you. You've been so kind and with me being a stranger."

"Somehow you don't seem like a stranger. More like family. And as family, I'm going to give you a hug for good luck."

We hugged and I said goodbye with a knot in my gut. I reached up, took hold of the pommel and pulled myself into the saddle. I lightly squeezed my legs against the side of my horse and we were off.

~~~~~~

I had been on the trail for two days when a scruffy looking man appeared out of the bushes right after I had set up camp and started a meal.

"Howdy stranger, that sure smells good. Could you spare a cup of coffee and a small plate of victuals?"
~~~~~~

"Sure, let me get another cup from my pack." As I reached Gertrude, I heard the cocking of a pistol. I will always be thankful to the wagon master, Mr. Shennagan and the scout, Mr. Green for their teaching of how to survive in the wilderness. I grabbed my rifle which was hanging on the pack, turned and fired. The stranger crumbled to the ground clutching his chest. I dropped my weapon and rushed to the fallen man. I kneeled down and listened for his breathing. There was none. He was dead.

"Oh dear Lord, you know I took no pleasure in taking this man's life. You know I had no choice. It was either him or me. Please forgive me."

I scraped out a shallow grave with the small shovel that Mrs. Ramsey had said might come in handy. I dropped the dead man into it and pushed the dirt in to cover the body. I, also, covered the grave with rocks to keep the varmints from digging up the body. I fashioned a cross from a couple of limbs and pushed it into the soft earth. Standing at the head of the grave, I again asked the Lord to forgive me and to take care of this stranger in the way He sees fit, whether it be a place in Heaven or a place in hell. Amen.

~~~~~~

After a filling meal of beans, bacon and coffee, I cleaned the dishes and spread my bed roll for the night. I stretched out on it, looked once more at the glorious sky, closed my eyes and fell immediately asleep. My dreams this night was very confusing and all jumbled together. I saw Nurse Thatcher bent over the dead man I had buried. She seemed to be mouthing the words, *how could you? How could you?*

I awoke the next morning, feeling not rested at all. I went in the business and took care of business, then went back and started a new fire. I retraced my steps from the night before and before long there was hot coffee to drink. I poured a cup, took a sip and again repeated last night by frying bacon and mixing in a can of beans. I would have enjoyed a breakfast of bacon and eggs, but alas there were no chickens to be found. I finished my breakfast, cleaned the dishes, packed them away in the bags. Thankfully there was plenty of lush green grass for the animals. I tied the sack that I had removed back on Gertrude, that's the name I gave the mule. I hadn't named the horse yet. All the names I thought about didn't
~~~~~~

seem fitting for such a magnificent animal. I was sure the appropriate one would come to me in time.

My thoughts wondered to Bearclaw, Moonglow, Nurse Thatcher, Doctor Montgomery and of course, Maggie Cole. I wonder if she went against her father's wishes and married the man she loved. I wish her a lifetime of happiness.

I tightened the cinch on my horse, grabbed the lead rope of the mule, climbed into the saddle and once again I was on my way. I settled myself into the saddle and looked up at the foreboding sight before me. The mountain looked even further away than it had yesterday. Perhaps my eyes were playing tricks on me. Surely, I had to be closer than I was yesterday. I made up my mind right then to ride all day without stopping for dinner and perhaps tomorrow, the mountain would look closer. I rode until the red-hot sun was hiding behind that mountain and stopped for the night.

I hadn't really been paying that much attention as I rode, so there wasn't a stream for this campsite. I hoped the two canteens held enough water for at least one cup of coffee. I needed it very badly. *What kind of grub did Mrs. Ramsey pack in these sacks? Come on, remember, you don't want to eat beans and bacon every meal, although I do enjoy them a lot.* I poured the cup of coffee I had brewed and proceeded to scrounge through the bags. I found several cans of different kinds of fruits and vegetables. I remembered some of the things the women on the wagon train had cooked on their journey. *I don't know if I will be able to produce things like, wait a minute, what's in this bag? It says rice. Do I have enough water?* I picked up both canteens and shook them. *Maybe just a small bowl of boiled rice with some sugar on it. Sure, that's what I'll do.* It was a new experience for me learning how close to set the pot to keep it from boiling the water away. I dumped a double handful of rice into the boiling water and it immediately boiled over the top. I, also, burned my hand when I forgot to use a rag to pick it up. After all the trouble I had cooking it, I enjoyed it very much. I thought of other things I might do with a bag of rice. *Rice and beans don't sound bad. Maybe mix in a little flour and have rice and dumplings.* My mind was racing with ideas. Then reality set in and I remembered where I was. And even though I might not be as green as I was at one time, I was still very much a greenhorn. I was so tired, I decided to clean up the mess in the morning. I checked on the horse and mule when I went to the bushes. They were still munching on the green grass oblivious to the long trip ahead of us. I spread my bed roll as close to the fire as I deemed necessary without getting burned. I remembered last night how the temperature had dropped once the sun disappeared from the sky. I didn't want to suffer like that tonight. I threw a couple of larger limbs on the fire and settled into my pallet.

I closed my eyes and the next thing I knew the sun was shining in my face. I squinted against the brightness and rolled out of bed. Then I remembered I had used all the water last night for my coffee and meal of boiled rice. *The next town I come to I need to purchase a barrel to carry water. I don't think a small barrel would be too much for Gertrude to handle. There's only one problem with my plan. How many towns or settlements are there between here and my destination? I really need to be more careful in the future or there might not be any future.*

I cleaned and packed the gear away, tightened the cinch and again pointed the horse toward the mountain. Was that pesky mountain moving or was I going crazy? I could swear it wasn't any closer now than it was yesterday morning. I rode again straight through without stopping, continually searching for any sign of that precious liquid that I and the animals needed. *There up ahead, what is that is it a pool of water?* As I drew closer, I realized it was only the sun reflecting on the ground. *Surely. I'm not suffering from lack of water this soon. I read some place one time a person can go for three days without water. Not as long as going without food, but a man can survive for a little while.* I set up straighter in the saddle when my horse raised his head and whinnied. He pulled on the reins as if he wanted me to follow him. I gave him his head and he led us to a small pool of clear cool refreshing liquid. The morning sun was casting a golden glow across the pond. I knew at that moment the name I was going to give my horse.

Golden Rod, (Goldy for short) because he had led us to this wonderful gift even more valuable than gold.

I slid from the saddle onto the ground, stumbled to the edge of the water, fell to my knees, then fell face first into the water. Drinking of this glorious nectar reminded me of that first drink of water Bearclaw gave me. I glanced up to see Goldy and Gertrude drinking as well. I raised up, resting on my haunches. I took a look around and found the small pond was surrounded by trees and bushes. A perfect place for a campsite. It would, also, be a great hiding place for someone on the run.

I stood and walked over to Gertrude and began unpacking and setting up camp. There would be plenty of water to experiment making different rice dishes tonight. I was quite excited about this new venture.

## CHAPTER EIGHT

After being in the saddle for six days, I reached the foothills of Echo Mountain. The directions Bearclaw had given were very easy to follow. It was a little after noon and I very tired, however, being this close seemed to perk me up, so I continued my journey.

~~~~~~

I arrived at the cabin of Bearclaw and Moonglow in the late afternoon. Bearclaw was scraping hides and stretching them onto boards, then hanging them on a line he had stretched between two poles. He didn't see and apparently didn't hear me as I rode up. I slid from my pony and walked toward him.

When I got about five feet from him, he whirled around looking ready to fight, then recognition registered on his face. "By golly, is it really you? You came jest like I hoped you would. My, my, it's good to see you. Come on, the old woman's gonna be mighty glad to see you. Come on."
~~~~~~

"I better take care of the animals. It's been a long trip and they been mighty good."

"You go on, I'll take care of 'em. You go on and surprise Moonglow."

I walked to the cabin, then hesitated. I wasn't sure about this. Maybe I'd better wait for the old man. I was standing in front of the door when it opened and I saw an old Indian woman, much older than I remembered.

"You come in, me make turnip soup for you." A big grin appeared on her face which brightened up the whole room. About that time, Bearclaw showed up and we all started talking at once. They wanted to know all about what I did after they left me at the clinic.

I told them about Nurse Thatcher, Doctor Montgomery and Maggie Cole. Tears filled my eyes as I told about Nurse Thatcher dying and how I had failed to tell her how I felt.

Moonglow touched my hand and said, "You young. Find somebody else. Make you happy."

<p style="text-align:center">~~~~~~</p>

I learned a lot from Bearclaw, mainly because he was a good teacher. He was very patient with me as I often made mistakes. "That's alright," he would say, "Lord knows I made my share of 'em. It'll get easier in time."

It had been a long trip from the orphanage to here where these two people felt like family. I enjoyed so much the evenings spent with Bearclaw and Moonglow, with them telling about all the years they had spent together and the many adventures of Bearclaw.

About three months after I arrived, Bearclaw said, "ya reckon ya know enough to run a line yer self?"

"You mean it?"

"Yeah, I figger ya can do it, be twice as many skins. You take the line we been working. I'll start a new one over to the East. Been watching it pretty close fer a couple of months. Now that yer here, I figger it's time."

~~~~~~

One day I asked him what his real name was. "Surely your mama didn't name you Bearclaw."
~~~~~~

"It's been so long I ain't sure I kin 'member it. Let's see now. I never did care for it while I was growing up. Kids all made fun of it. Onie Flannery, yep, kin you believe a name like Onie?"

"It ain't so bad. I've heard worse. Where'd you get that necklace you wear?"

"Killed the bear they belonged to. Was quite a battle too."

"I'd like to hear about it."

"Another time, we need to get going or we won't make it back in time for supper, and you don't want to be late, now do you?"

I had been late only one time and Moonglow let me know about it. I vowed then and there that I wouldn't be late again. Not if I could help it.

Bearclaw taught me how to tan hides and how to make moccasins and other things. I would never have guessed urine was used in the process. Soaking the hides in urine made it easier to remove the hair and made it easy to work with. I was surprised at quite a few things that he taught me.

Urine was, also, used to trap animals. Just a dab around the trap would entice a varmint to get caught. It seemed there was something new each day for me to learn.

~~~~~~

A few days later I asked again if he would tell me how he got the name Bearclaw.

"It happened just a little after first light. I was almost ready to head home. Had a pretty fair catch. Of course, we always wish it was better. Anyhow, I was pulling the trap outta the water when a bear cub hunkered up beside me. Now, just a cub ain't nothing to worry about long as the mama ain't around, but on this day, Mama was watching baby close and she didn't like me messing with the little one, which I wasn't, but that didn't matter none. She raised up on her hind legs and let me tell you she was a big one. Close to seven feet tall and mad. I wish I could've talked bear right about then, but the only thing I could do was get ready to fight for my life. You know the worst thing you can do is run from a bear, anyhow this
~~~~~~

mama wasn't gonna let me run, so, I grabbed my Bowie and my tomahawk.

Those was the only weapons I had to take on this seven foot giant. I took a swing with my tomahawk; it barely touched her nose which only made her madder. She was extremely fast for such a large creature. She was on me before I had a chance to do anything and we fell to the ground. It was all I could do to keep those enormous teeth away from my throat. I had my tomahawk in one hand and the Bowie in the other. When she reared her head back, I saw an opening and thrust my knife into her throat. It was like an ocean of blood flooded over me. And then I was finding it hard to breathe because she fell straight down on me.

I lay still for a minute or two saying a prayer to the good Lord for sparing my life. It was a struggle, but I managed to pull myself free of that weight. I rolled over and got to my feet, taking a big breath and again thanking God. The cub was sniffing Mama Bear and making a whimpering noise. "I'm sorry Baby, but I didn't have a choice." I picked the baby up and headed home. I'd have to come back later and skin the mama. We raised that cub till it was old enough to make it on its own, then we turned it loose into the wild. These are the teeth from that mama bear that I wear around my neck to remind me of that day."

~~~~~~

We ran two trap lines from then on until Bearclaw told me one day that he wanted me to stay close to the cabin. "Just in case," as he put it, without finishing the sentence.

"Why?" I asked.

"The old woman ain't been acting like herself lately. I'm jest a little worried about her. Can you do that fer me?"

"Sure, there's plenty of hides to be scraped."

"Thanks Son, it means a lot to me."

I stayed around close to the cabin, doing small jobs like chopping wood and other piddling jobs. Then one day shortly after breakfast, we heard an awful noise.

"That sound like Old Man, you go see."
~~~~~~

I made my way to the east side of the mountain. That's where Bearclaw had set his traps last week. I hadn't been going with him as usual.

I had just come out of the bushes when I saw the bear. It was still hunched over Bearclaw. I could see even from this distance Bearclaw was dead. I raised my rifle and fired, the slug entered the animal's head and it slumped down onto Bearclaw.

I rushed over, laying my rifle on the ground, I tried pulling the dead bear off my friend's body, but it was too heavy, I would have to bring the mule back. Walking back to the cabin was one of the longest walks I had ever made. Moonglow was standing in the yard as I walked up. I looked at her and shook my head. She bowed her head and fell to her knees rocking back and forth. A slow wail came from her and then turned into an agonizing scream.

I didn't know what to do or how to help her, so I turned and got the mule with a length of rope and headed back to get my friend.

It didn't take long to pull the bear off Bearclaw's body. The bear had really done a job on him. He was mutilated pretty badly. His face was almost unrecognizable. There was no way I was gonna let Moonglow see him like this, however, she had a different idea about that. I loaded his body onto the mule and headed to the cabin.

Moonglow was waiting and told me to carry him inside. She had me lay Bearclaw's body on their bed, then she asked me to leave them alone while she prepared the body for burial. I learned later that Indians have a different view about life and death.

"You go to big tree up yonder and dig grave. He will be ready by time you finish, then you come back to take him."

I did as she asked and sure enough, just like she said, he was ready. His body was completely wrapped in a bear skin. Moonglow handed me the bear claw necklace that was always around the neck of her husband of many years. "He wanted you to have necklace. You son we never had."

We loaded Bearclaw's body on a travois and walked to the tree that he had liked so much. He had spent many hours sitting under that tree. He said on many occasions. "This is one of the many things I love about these mountains. It's so peaceful here, why would anybody want to live anyplace else?"

## CHAPTER NINE

Almost immediately after burying Bearclaw, Moonglow said she wanted to leave to go back to her people on the other side of the mountain. She said Bearclaw always promised her they would go, but it never happened.

It was a hard and tedious journey to cross the top of the mountain this time of year.

"Now, we go now, you take me. Make animals ready for long journey. Load packs in shed on animals. Trip take many moons."

I got the feeling that she wasn't gonna change her mind. We were going.

Moonglow had started packing right away. I had always thought she was kinda slow, because of her age, but I was wrong. She was moving like someone more than half her age.

"You load packs on animals.?"

"Yes, they're all loaded. I think we should wait until tomorrow. It's getting kinda late to be starting such a long journey, don't you think?"

"We go now. Tomorrow may be too late."

"What'd you mean by that?"

"No matter, we go now. Hurry, be ready soon."

It was a little afternoon when we started. "Are you sure you want to start now? I think it would be better to start first thing in the morning."

"No wait. We go now. Maybe you no wanna go. It okay, go self. No need young man who fuss all time."

"I said I would go and I will. It's just...."

"If you go, then we go."

So, exactly one day after the death of Bearclaw, me and Moonglow started a journey to her people on the other side of the mountain.

Every time I slowed just a little, Moonglow would holler for me to hurry, "you hurry, we got long way to go."

The sun began to settle behind the horizon as we had just reached the first trail heading further up the mountain. There was a small clearing with a little stream, a very good place for a campsite.

"We make camp here. Morning come early. You take care of animals, I make camp. I good make camp, cook something to eat. You fill canteens."

I had always thought Moonglow was a very good cook, but I think she was even better at cooking over an open fire. How she made the meal taste so good was a mystery to me.

There were quite a few meals and each one seemed to taste better than the last.

We did eat a lot of pemmican; this was an Indian's jerky.

<center>~~~~~~</center>

We met a small band of Indians the seventh day out. Moonglow said, "Me talk. You be still. Not talk 'less me say talk."

It was a scary time. The only time I had seen any Indians other than Bearclaw and Moonglow was when the wagon train was attacked and I almost died.

Moonglow raised her hand and said, "we go to camp of Chief Washita. Chief my brother. We want no trouble with Chickasaw. You let us pass."

"Why you let old woman speak for you? Are you afraid? Do you have tongue or has big cat eat tongue?" He directed this to me, using hand signs along with broken English.

"Say nothing," Moonglow said quietly, so they couldn't hear. "You make big talk to crazy one. Him have Great Spirit protect him. You no want upset Great Spirit."

The leader glanced around at the other warriors, then back at me. "Him no look crazy."

"Why you think him let old woman speak for him?"

"We go. Leave crazy one to travel our land." The warriors all turned and headed away from the trail.

"What did you say to them?"

"Me tell'em you crazy and Great Spirit protect."

"Why'd you tell them that? I ain't crazy."

"Them not know that. Now they leave us alone. We be safe travels now."

We met several different Indians, but were able to talk to them and persuade them that we meant no harm to them or their hunting ground. Soon, word of our traveling reached all the tribes and we weren't approached any more.

~~~~~~

"We go this way," said Moonglow. "It much shorter."

"I thought we were going to the other side of the mountain. Shouldn't we keep going up?"

"This shorter way. We go shorter way. You follow."

I fell in behind Moonglow's horse, wondering if she knew where we were going. Had she become confused in her old age?

After a few miles we came upon a narrow passage probably a hundred yards alongside the edge of a cliff.

"Be careful, hold tight on horses, fall off, no good."
~~~~~~

"No kidding," I said.

It was barely wide enough for the horses.

"Get off now, lead horses."

I watched as Moonglow dismounted and started leading her horse. Rocks started falling where the horse's hooves were coming close to the edge. She made it seemingly easy. She waved and shouted, "you come now. Easy, you see."

I took the reins of one of the pack horses and began what Moonglow had proclaimed to be easy. It was easy enough for the two pack animals, but when I started out with Goldy, his left hoof slipped on a stone and he almost went over. Thankfully he regained his footing and we made it to the other side.

"I sure don't want to do that again," I said, wiping my face with my bandanna.

"No do again, no necessary. Now we make better time."

~~~~~~
~~~~~~

After four more days, a blizzard seemed to come out of nowhere. "We go this way, there is cave."

"How do you know there's a cave."

"Remember from when I was young, hurry, it get colder soon. Freeze animals. Cave not far."

Sure enough, there was a cave off to the right of the trail. It was large enough for the animals, so we rode right inside.

"Hurry, get tarps from packs. Cover opening, quick now."

Moonglow's survival pack had enough things to outfit an army. She had perfected cooking over a fire perfectly. I don't believe she fixed anything that wasn't delicious. Also, there was plenty of debris and wood inside the enclosure to keep the fire fueled. Moonglow explained that when we left, we would replenish what we had used so the next traveler that found themselves in the cave wouldn't have to be scrounging for material to build a fire.

I had never seen a woman as old as Moonglow work so fast. In no time at all she had the packs off the animals and a fire started.

"You hurry, cover opening with tarps, storm only get worse. Horses need saddles off."

I finished covering the opening and began removing the saddles. As I laid them close to the fire, I saw a coffee pot giving a delightful aroma and a skillet filled with something that smelled really good.

"How did you know about this cave?"

"Me tell you. Remember from when young like you. People travel this way many times. People always leave plenty wood for fire. We leave plenty wood when leave."

"That's a real nice thing to do. Helping weary travelers."

One morning, when I woke, I felt something laying against me. It felt like a slick bag. When I moved, I learned it wasn't a bag, when I heard the rattlingly.

"Moonglow," I said quietly. "There's a rattlesnake in my bed."

"You lay still, no move." Then, she like started singing. I've never seen anything like it. It was just like I seen in the picture books with the snake charmer. That snake crawled from under my blanket and crawled right toward Moonglow's voice. When it got about three feet from her, she threw her knife and severed that snake's head. That was our morning meal and a very good meal."

We had just finished eating when the tarp broke loose, and the snow started blowing in. I jumped up and started fastening it again to cover the opening.

"It must be below freezing out there. It's a good thing you remembered this cave or we'd be in real trouble."

"We be in big trouble if run outta wood. Long way to more wood."

"Well, we'll just have to be careful with what we have."

We could hear the wind howling like a runaway freight train.

"How long does a storm last?"

"Last as long as it lasts," she said. "Great Spirit in charge. Not get in hurry sometime."

Well, the Great Spirit didn't hurry this time. The storm raged on for five days, then on the sixth, it stopped. It was an almost eerie feeling to not hear the noise of the blowing wind.

"Storm stop, we chop wood for next traveler." She started packing up the gear. "Saddle horses. We go as soon as replace wood. Take down tarp."

We had to walk almost a mile to find enough trees to chop for wood to replace what we had used. After that task was completed, we got back on the trail. I noticed we were still going uphill. And here I thought we were at the top. As if she heard my thoughts, Moonglow said, "we be going down real soon."

We had just finished setting up camp and was enjoying a cup of coffee when the horses began to act nervous and pulling at their reins. I jumped up to quite them down when I saw what was causing them to be afraid. There just beyond the firefight were three or four wolves.

"Throw piece of meat. They just hungry."

She handed me a slab of bacon. Then said, "hold it so they can see it." Then just like with the snake she started singing. The big wolf that seemed to be the leader stopped in his tracks and cocked his head to the side as if his ears were hurting or he was listening to Moonglow's singing. "Now, throw meat."

I did as she asked, but the wolves stood still. The leader still had his head cocked to the side. Moonglow stopped singing and the leader straightened his head and stepped forward, grabbed the slab of bacon, turned and walked away with the others following.

Moonglow then said, we eat now, they not come back."

## CHAPTER TEN

It seemed as if Moonglow had slowed in her actions since the time we spent in the cave and I lost my patience with her on more than one occasion. But I apologized after each blowup. She said she understood the impatience of a young man such as myself and she said she knew what I was going through. She remembered when her husband was my age, how he on many occasions would become so irritated with her, he threatened to return her to her people. But then, he would always say how sorry he was and hug her. She would regale me with stories of when she and the old man were young. Like me, he was what was called a greenhorn. He knew nothing of how to survive, but he refused to go back to a civilization where folks made fun of him for marrying an Indian. They called him Squawman and her a filthy dog eating squaw. From that time on, the only human contact they had was with other Indians and other whites at rendezvous. Those were happy times because those men were like them.

~~~~~~

After traveling for almost four more weeks, we reached a valley. A beautiful valley with lush green grass and trees with a winding river running through it.

"This be it, my people's village."

"It's beautiful." I said.

As we rode down into the valley, four braves showed up and rode alongside us.

As we entered the village, the women and children stood watching us. After several tepees, an elderly Indian stepped out of a teepee and raised his hand in greeting. "Welcome sister, it has been many moons. Please enter teepee and share drink. Bring crazy one who is protected by Great Spirit."

"How does he know all that?" I asked.

"Our coming has been known from first day we leave."

We dismounted and followed the chief inside the teepee. The first thing I noticed, after I got used to the
~~~~~~

darkness, was how much room there was, much more than it seemed from the outside.

Chief Washita sat in front of the fire and motioned for us to sit, also. After we were settled, a young maiden handed us a bowl with a sweet aroma to it. I watched Moonglow to see what she did, so I wouldn't make any mistakes. I lifted the bowl to my lips, just as she did and was pleased with the taste of the liquid.

Next, the same young maiden brought us another bowl filled with some sort of soup or broth. The aroma was intoxicating. And it was just as delicious as the smell.

"I have heard of the death of your man." The chief said. "He was a good and honorable man. I share in your loss and your pain. I am only sorry it took the death of Bearclaw for you to return to your people."

"The people have always been in my thoughts, and you, also, my brother."

I hadn't really been paying attention to the young maiden when she brought the bowls of nourishment, but as she stood behind the chief, I got a really good look at her. She was one of the most beautiful women I had ever seen. I felt something I hadn't felt since Nurse Thatcher.

"You must be tired after your journey, please allow my granddaughter to take you to your teepee. We will visit more after you rest."

We stood and followed the young woman out of the teepee. She led us to another teepee with the markings of a chief. How I knew this was because Moonglow told me.

"Perhaps you will share your journey with me?" She asked looking at Moonglow.

"Me tired, young man not. He share with you." She looked at me and winked.

I will have to admit, I was a little apprehensive about being alone with this beautiful young woman, especially after the feeling I had when I first saw her.

"You seem a bit nervous." She said, looking up at me with the greenest eyes. *Are Indians supposed to have green eyes?*

"I suppose I am, a little." I answered. "You speak vary good English."

"My father was a trapper; a white man and I attended the school at Fort Anderson when I was very young. My mother was killed when I was very young and my father left, so I was raised by my grandmother. Please tell me your name and about your journey."

"My name is Jarod Marsh. There's really not much to tell, just a normal trip. And what is your name?"

"My name is Morning Flower. I am called Flower. I understand you were considered to be crazy, what was that about?"

"We met a small group of Chickasaw. Moonglow thought it would be best to do the talking and told them I was crazy and protected by the Great Spirit."

"What else?" She asked, with excitement in her voice.

"Well, we had to wait out a blizzard in a cave."

"It all sounds so exciting. What else?"

"There was these wolves. It was the oddest thing the way Moonglow sang to them and it was like they were hypnotized. I tossed a slab of bacon to them. Normally, if a wolf is hungry, he won't let anything keep him from a meal, but they all waited until Moonglow stopped singing. It really was something to see."

"It sounds so exciting; I wish I could have been there."

"It does sound exciting when I tell it, but I have to say, it wasn't exciting at the time, it was just plain old scary."

"What else, please tell me more." The excitement showing in her voice.

"There was another time in the cave when I had a little problem with a snake, a rattlesnake. I woke early one morning when I felt something in my bedroll. I knew immediately what it was."

Moonglow looked and heard the snake's rattle, she saw I had a big problem. "You lay still, no move." Then, just like she did with the wolves, she started singing. I've never seen anything like it. It was just like I seen in the picture books with the snake charmer. That snake crawled from under my blanket and crawled right toward

Moonglow's voice. When it got about three feet from her, she threw her knife and severed that snake's head. That was our morning meal and a very good meal."

"I'll say it over and over, I wish I only had such exciting things in my life."

"Surely you have had some excitement. It don't look boring here."

"I suppose for an outsider it might seem exciting, but for someone who lives here, it is the same thing day after day."

"Don't you have a special place where you like to be alone?"

"I do, would you like to join me?"

"I asked if it was a place you like to be alone."

"I would like to share it with you."

"Okay, let's go."

She led me out beyond the teepee area.

"Be careful, there are guards. Come this way." She took my hand and a thrill rushed through me. As we got further away from the village the forest hid us from anyone that would be looking for us. We walked for almost a half hour.

"We're almost there, I just know you're going to like this place as much as I do."

~~~~~~

"Well, what do you think?"

There in front of us was a waterfall, three waterfalls, in fact. And a beautiful pond at the bottom.

"It's wonderful and beautiful just like you."

She blushed and smiled, "I just knew you would like it."

"How long have you been coming here?"

"A few years, since I was fifteen, right after I returned from the school at Fort Anderson. When I discovered it, I knew it was a special place to only be shared with a special someone."

"So, you think I'm special?"

"Oh yes, I do. Perhaps you think me forward, but I've always been taught to follow my heart."
~~~~~~

"I feel the same about you. I've only felt like this one other time, but it wasn't meant to be."

"Please tell me about her, if you don't mind?"

"On my way to California in a wagon train, we were attacked and I was wounded very badly. She was the nurse that took care of me, her name was Thatcher, Nurse Thatcher. I really can't explain why I was attracted to her, but I was. She was killed before I could share how I felt about her."

"I am so sorry. We should be getting back; Grandfather will be wondering where I am."

She held out her hand for me and I gladly took it in mine and we walked back to the village. Just as we got to the edge of the village, a young brave stepped in front of us, I noticed that he was looking at us holding hands and he didn't look happy.

"Where you go? I look for you and you not here."

"I don't need to tell you everything."

"You go place with white eyes?"

"And what if I did? It's none of your business."

"Your grandfather promise we be married."

"My grandfather said he would consider it; he didn't say it was a sure thing."

"You like crazy one much?"

"He's not crazy and yes I like him."

"I hear from others, he crazy. Old woman say it is so."

"She said that so the other tribes would leave them alone. He is not crazy."

"Look," I said. "I think you should go away. It looks like you're upsetting Flower."

"Who are you to think you speak for her?"

"I'm the one who is going to stop you from upsetting her."

"Stop! Both of you. Standing Bear, I am asking you nicely, please go now."

"I will go as you say, for now, but I tell you this is not the end. I do not care for this white eyes." He turned and walked away.

"I apologize for Standing Bear's rudeness. He has some stupid idea that I belong to him, because my grandfather told him he would consider him for my husband."

"Perhaps we should not be seen together. I wouldn't want to cause trouble."

"There won't be any trouble. Unless you don't want to see me again."

"I definitely want to see you again, that is, if you do."

"Yes, I do. But right now, I must hurry, my grandfather will be worried about me. I'll see you later, okay?"

"Yes, goodbye until later."

I watched until she was out of sight, then I turned and went to the teepee where Moonglow was.

"You have good time with Flower?" she asked as I entered.

"I really like her; I hope that's alright. I don't know the customs of your people."

"If customs mean something, Bearclaw and Moonglow never be together. My father not want me marry Bearclaw, but we in love, disobey Father. This why we live other side mountain. We sleep now, morning come early."

~~~~~~

Yes, the morning did come early, at least for me. For some reason I overslept. My face was hot and I had an awful headache. Moonglow felt my forehead and proclaimed, "you have fever, stay in blanket, I fix medicine for you, feel better soon."

When Standing Bear learned I had a fever, he shouted to the entire village, "white eyes bring sickness to our village. Before long all be sick like him."

The medicine man showed up and did some blowing smoke and rattling some beads over me and declared everything was gonna be okay.

In the meantime, Moonglow had used herbs from her medicine bag and brewed up a concoction and had me drink it. She, also, rubbed a smelly substance on my chest. Before long I was feeling much better.
~~~~~~

"You stay in bed until tomorrow. Be like new then."

~~~~~~

Sure enough, the next morning, I felt as if I had never been sick.

"What was in that stuff you had me drink?" I asked Moonglow.

"Secret." She said and winked.

~~~~~~

I was walking alone around the camp when I was approached by Standing Bear. "Are you feeling better now. Strong enough to go on hunt? You must be good hunter, trained by old woman's man."

"I reckon I'm a fair hunter."

"Come, we go." He turned, expecting me to follow.

I followed him as four others joined us. I had an uneasy feeling about this, however, I continued to follow him.

"Are we going hunting without weapons?" I asked as the other braves surrounded me. "What's wrong Standing

Bear, are you afraid to fight me yourself? Do you need help?"

"I no afraid, my friends are here to keep you from running away."

~~~~~~

When we were a few miles from camp, we ran into a band of Chickasaw braves and a white man. "What you doing away from village?" The leader asked. "And why you have crazy one with you?"

"This our land, you not belong here. Must leave now." Standing Bear told him.

"You not hear, why crazy one with you? Where old woman who speak for him?"

"I can speak for myself. I need no-one to speak for me."

"You not sound crazy. Sound plenty smart. You are smart, that be true, yes?"

"Smart enough I reckon. How about you, are you smart?"
~~~~~~

"Me smart like wise owl. That why I am called White Owl. Me think you smart like White Owl, yes?"

"Hold on, jest a minute." Said the white man. "You told me we'd not have no trouble. So, why don't we all jest take a step back? We can be friendly, can't we? Is old Chief Rushing Bird still the chief here?" He asked, looking first at me and then Standing Bear.

"Who are you, asking about Chief Rushing Bird?" Standing Bear asked.

"His daughter was my wife."

"Why you here?"

"I told you, The chief's my father-in-law. I've come for my daughter, Summer Flower."

"What you mean, come for daughter."

"Jest that, I'm her father and I've come fer her. I want her to come with me, I've got a husband for her."

In the meantime, the Chickasaw braves began leaving. "We leave, too many crazy white eyes." Exclaimed the leader, as they rode away.

## CHAPTER ELEVEN

The saloon was semi-dark and dusty. Five men sat at a table in the back. A man with a white beard and shoulder length hair, approximately forty years old was sweating profusely. As he wiped his brow with a dirty bandanna, he said in a trembling voice, "Surely we can work something out?"

"Perhaps we can. Rumor has it you lived with the Indians for a while. Is that just a rumor, or is it true?"

"It's true, even had me a Injun wife. But when she died, I skedaddled outta there. Why you asking?"

"I've got a hankering for some young Indian squaw. I reckon if you could maybe fix me up with a young squaw, we could call it even."

"Sure, I can do that. You saying that's all I have to do? Bring a squaw to you and I won't owe you no more?"

"That is correct. You'll be free and clear. However, I do expect the squaw to be pretty."

"Yes sir, she will be. Very pretty."

# CHAPTER TWELVE

One day Moonglow wanted to show me a special place, so we rode out of camp. The scenery was beautiful. Lush green grass and trees everywhere. I thought where Moonglow and Bearclaw lived was beautiful, but this was breathtaking. All that green against a cloudless blue sky.

Then as if the sky heard my thoughts, dark clouds filled the sky. "We need find shelter quick. Be bad storm."

There was a stand of cottonwoods just ahead. "We go there." She said, pointing toward the trees.

By now, large drops of rain were coming down hard, then the rain turned to hail. The cottonwoods made a good covering that blocked out most of the hail.

"We sure was lucky these cottonwoods were here. That hail would've sure beat us up pretty bad."

"Great Spirit watch over us, all time."

"You really believe that don't you?"

"Me believe. You, also."

"Maybe sometimes, other times, I just don't know."

"We go now. Rain stop. Ice from sky stop. We hurry, be dark soon. Long way to special place."

"We could stay here, get early start in the morning."

"No, we go special place now. Not wait morning."

"What's so special about this other campsite?"

"You see, very special, good place. Come we hurry."

We rode until the moon was high in the sky. "How much further is this place?"

"Almost there. Be patient. You will like place."

Sure enough, as we rode over a small rise, there it was. A small valley with a waterfall and a pond.

"It's beautiful," I said with excitement in my voice.

"This place where I meet Bearclaw first time. I look him and he look me. Love for both forever. Special place for old woman."

"I can see why it's a special place. What was Bearclaw doing on this side of the mountain?"

"Him come trap for beaver, say no beaver where he come from. Him look me, me look him. Fall love then forever."

"You said your father didn't approve of Bearclaw. What was it that he didn't like?"

"Him not like white men. Kill his father and brother. Him much bitter many year."

"So, you and Bearclaw left and didn't come back, even after your father died?"

"Me want to, old man promise, many moon pass, but no happen. 'Til now."

"Wait a minute, this looks exactly like Flower's special place, but I didn't think it was this far from the village."

"Maybe I take long way." Said Moonglow. "Maybe Flower know short way. You maybe like Flower, yes?"

"Maybe," told her. "Just don't know how she feels about me."

"What she tell you?"

"She says she cares, but I just don't know. don't have any experience with women."

"What this experi....?"

"It means I've not been around many women."

"Me no know this experi.., just know how heart feels. How your heart feel? She tell you she care for you, listen to heart."

"But what if she don't feel the same?"

"Not know if not tell. Come we go back village. You tell her then."

## CHAPTER THIRTEEN

As we rode into the village, we noticed a big commotion. As we got closer, we saw an older white man in an argument with the chief. Their voices were very loud.

"You not take Morning Flower. You left her many moons ago. She is no longer your daughter."

"We'll see about that. I'm her father and I say she's coming with me."

Standing Bear had been standing silently to the side. "I will fight white man for Summer Flower. It is my right as War Chief."

"I ain't gonna fight nobody to take my own flesh and blood with me."

"You fight. You win. Take Summer Flower. You lose, you leave, no come back here no more."

"What's happening?" I asked Moonglow.

"White man Summer Flower's real father. Him want take Flower away."

"I can't let that happen. I gotta do something."

"Maybe you do something. Make challenge to white man like Standing Bear."

"Can I do that?"

"Yes, tell Chief you wish to fight white man for right to marry Summer Flower."

"But Standing Bear has already challenged the white man."

"I know my brother. He does not like Standing Bear. May be, he like you better. Make challenge."

I stepped in front of Standing Bear and said to the chief, "I challenge this white man for the hand of Summer Flower."

"No!" Shouted Standing Bear. "He is, also, white man. This is a trick."

"No trick. I love Summer Flower and want to marry her, if I have to do battle with whoever to do this, I'm more than willing to do so."

"You have my permission to challenge this white man."

"Hang on. Just wait a minute. I ain't agreeing to this. I'm gonna just take my daughter and go and there ain't nobody gonna stop me."

"I'll stop you," I said loudly. "The only way you'll take her is over my dead body. Now what's it gonna be?"

You could see the sweat rolling down his face and his eyes were darting back and forth like a scared animal. He looked at the chief, then at me and said, "no way, I ain't fighting nobody. You're welcome to her." Then he turned, ran to his horse and rode outta the village.

Flower came running from behind her grandfather right into my arms. "I was so afraid you were going to be hurt. What made you do that?"

"I thought it would be pretty plain to you. I told your grandfather that I loved you and wanted to marry you, so what do you say? Will you marry me?"

"Oh yes, I will marry you. I love you with all my heart."

I looked at Moonglow. Her face was beaming with a big smile and then she winked at me.

All the people were murmuring amongst themselves. Chief Washita held up his hand for silence. "We will have the ceremony tomorrow."

Standing Bear stood in front of the chief. "I demand satisfaction, Summer Flower is supposed to be my bride. You promised, Chief Washita, you promised."

"I only told you I would consider you if Summer Flower excepted you. She has chosen this man."

"I will fight for her. I will destroy this white eyes and then she will be mine."

Flower spoke up. "You may fight this white eyes and win, but you will never win my heart. It belongs to this man and will forever. You need to realize this."

Standing Bear hung his head in defeat. "I will let you go because I care so much for you."

**EPLOGUE**

Jarod and Flower were married. Their first child was born the same day that Moonglow died.

Standing Bear and I became good friends when I carried him back to the village after a bad accident. Because of this we became blood brothers

Moonglow had told me that when she died, she wanted to be buried beside Bearclaw.

"You promise take old woman home. Bury next to husband. You promise," her breath left her body and she was gone. Tears filled my eyes as I remembered what Moonglow had meant to me. She was like a mother to me. She and Bearclaw were my family.

A few days after Moonglow died, Flower and I loaded her body on a travois and headed to the other side of Echo Mountain.

## J.C. Hulsey Books
## is a family-oriented organization.

What I mean by that is, we as a family will help one another in all aspects of our work. Now we all know that families squabble, fuss and might even come to fisticuffs at times, but if someone jumps on one of the members of our family, then they have to take on all of us. We may not like one another at times, but when we get to the bottom line, we do care about and love one another.

That's all fine, you may say, but it doesn't really tell me what J.C. Hulsey Books is going to do for me to make my book a success.

If you are a Western Writer that often feels as if no one cares. If you feel overlooked and discounted? If you feel like you aren't getting the credit that you deserve?

Well, don't think you are the only one who has those feelings. Western novelist quite often do not get the credit they deserve.

But in today's new world of publishing, Western Books have the potential to become one of the leading sellers in today's book market. Your story could very well be the one at the top of the best sellers list with the help of J.C. Hulsey Books.

J.C. Hulsey Books has the experience, the expertise, the contacts and the power to put your Western Novel at the top of the best sellers list J.C. Hulsey Books believes Western Authors have HUGE potential J.C. Hulsey Books is looking for Western writers to join our rapidly growing family of successful authors.

Make the move today to J.C. Hulsey Books.

Join the growing ranks of Western writers looking for success by hanging your spurs in the stable at J.C. Hulsey Books.